E V E   B U N T I N G

Peepers

Illustrated by
James Ransome

HARCOURT, INC.

San Diego   New York   London

Library of Congress Cataloging-in-Publication Data
Bunting, Eve, 1928– .
Peepers/Eve Bunting; illustrated by James Ransome.
p.   cm.
Summary: While helping their dad run Fred's Fall Color Tours in New England, Jim and Andy
think the tourists are pretty silly; then one night the boys experience something that makes them
change their minds.
[1. Fall foliage—Fiction.   2. Tourism—Fiction.   3. Autumn—Fiction.   4. New England—
Fiction.]   I. Ransome, James, ill.   II. Title.
PZ7.B91527Pd   2001
[Fic]—dc21   99-6292
ISBN 0-15-260297-6

H G F E D C B

Manufactured in China

The paintings in this book were done in acrylics on paper.
The display type was set in Rio Grande.
The text type was set in Minion.
Color separations by Bright Arts Ltd., Hong Kong
Manufactured by South China Printing Company, Ltd., China
This book was printed on totally chlorine-free
Nymolla Matte Art paper.
Production supervision by Sandra Grebenar and
Pascha Gerlinger
Designed by Ivan Holmes

For my son Sloan, who loves nature

—E. B.

To my New England family: the Clines and the Sneeds,
especially Uncle Stinky

—J. R.

In fall my dad opens up the shed where our little green bus sits waiting. Jim and I help him take off the blankets we piled on it last winter. The bus says FRED'S FALL COLOR TOURS on the side.

"Sparkle it up, boys," Dad orders. "The Leaf Peepers are coming."

The Peepers are what we call the tourists who come in the fall to see our bright-colored trees. In October Dad has Peeper bookings for every day. Now that Jim and I are a year older, we have to go along to help on weekends. We'd argue, but what's the use? Weekends mean full buses, and Dad can't do it alone.

Our bus crawls slow as a caterpillar along the quiet roads. Every time Dad stops, the Peepers get out and take pictures of the bright red sugar maples and the shagbark hickory trees.

"Oh," they say. "Look! Look, how beautiful!"

Jim and I call that "Peeper talk." When they can't see me, I point to a spilled-over trash can.

"Oh, look!" I whisper. "Look, how beautiful."

Jim about busts laughing.

"Want a picture of the pond?" Dad asks the Peepers.

"Sure do, Fred," they chorus. Dad's name isn't Fred. He bought the bus from Fred Jenkins.

The pond is ringed with speckled alder and red-feathered sumac. Aspens shower gold into the water. A beaver pops up, making a circle of ripples.

"Oh!" the Peepers say. "Look! Look, how beautiful!"

Jim and I roll our eyes. But we're looking, too, because beavers don't pop up that often.

Dad stops at the old Clements graveyard. It's small and only
Clementses are buried there. There's Mr. Clements, and his wife, Suzanne,
who died in 1772. SWEETLY REST, the tombstone says. There are
umpteen little Clements children, their places marked with slates, like
crooked teeth. It would be sad except it's so long ago.

Beeches and quaking aspens bend above the gravestones.

"Like blessings," a woman says.

Jim and I play leapfrog over the children's markers.

"Boys! Boys!" Dad warns. "Show some respect."

He drives us down to the river.

Leaves float like toy boats. They make a pile in the quiet water by the bridge. Jim and I call it Leaf Island. But you can't stand on it. We've tried.

It's almost Halloween. Mom has propped dried cornstalks against our porch. Pumpkins litter the fields around town, hundreds and thousands of them.

"They're the color of the leaves," a Peeper says. "Or else the leaves are the color of the pumpkins."

Straw scarecrows keep watch. One is playing a guitar. The Peepers pose with him. One pretends to sing along, her arm around his shoulders. Her husband takes a picture.

"What a ham!" I whisper.

The road sign reads MOOSE CROSSING.

But the moose are not obliging.

"Promises, promises," the Peepers say.

Dad gives out copies of pictures we took one night. A moose stands in the road next to the sign. It's as if we'd arranged him there. He is humongous, and the flash from the camera puts fire in his eyes.

"Moose only come down at dusk," Dad explains. "All you see in the headlights are four legs and a big black shadow."

"Oh my," the Peepers say. "Fancy that!"

Behind their backs Jim moose-prances and makes antlers with his fingers.

The leaves are fading now.

A few cling to the top branches, sigh, and drop, one by one.

The flat roof of our porch is as heavy with leaves as it will be with snow. The reds and golds are all mixed together.

A few leaves sail through the air like butterflies. They rest awhile and paint their shapes on the sidewalks so we'll remember them.

It's getting really cold. One morning the bus is stiff with frost.
The shops that sell antiques and cherishables are closed.
The tour phone has stopped ringing.

"Season's gone," Dad says. "Peepers, too."

"Promises, promises," we say happily.

"Time to put the bus back in the shed," Dad tells us, and eases it in.

Jim and I check between the seats for lost Peeper money while we're cleaning. We've lucked out a couple of times. There's none today.

We pile on the blankets.

"She sleeps here all winter like an old black bear," Dad says.

Of course, the bus is the wrong color, but that's all right.

Jim and I close the shed doors and grin.

We're free.

One night we put on our jackets and go out in the backyard. The leaves all blew away in the last big wind. Jim and I figure there's a leaf planet somewhere that they fly to. How else could they disappear so fast?

Our trees poke their branches, black and spiky, against the sky.

"Like brooms, sweeping the clouds," Jim says. He sounds embarrassed.

He *should* be embarrassed.

The stars are crackling cold.

The moon is as big as a pumpkin.

I guess our winter sky is always like this, but I just never noticed. I'm seeing it now the way the Peepers would see it.

I point up, and I'm embarrassed, too. But what the heck!

"Look!" I say. "Look, how beautiful!"